# To Rosie and John

Scholastic Children's Books,
Commonwealth House,
1-19 New Oxford Street,
London WC1A 1NU, UK
a division of Scholastic Ltd
London ~ New York ~ Toronto ~ Sydney ~ Auckland
Mexico City ~ New Delhi ~ Hong Kong

First published by Scholastic Ltd, 1999

Copyright © Tim Archbold, 1999

ISBN 0 590 11422 0

Printed in China

# WHAT'S THAT NOISE?

## Tim Archbold

SCHOLASTIC
PRESS

# Hurrah weeeeoo

wooopeee hurra

ah ha ha hoo ha ha fiz

What is that noise?
It's popping and whizzing.
It's giggling and hooting
And slurping and fizzing!

# a yum yum tooo

No!
Let's go and see.
Run, run, follow me!

# mmm weeee toot t

Is it something creeping
Underneath the floor?
Something really scary
With a frightening roar?

ing doo daa plink

What is that noise?
Is it parrots squawking?
Or a dinosaur walking?
Alarm bells ringing?
Or stray cats singing?
An elephant sneezing?
A steam engine wheezing?
A hurricane . . . ?
An aeroplane . . . ?

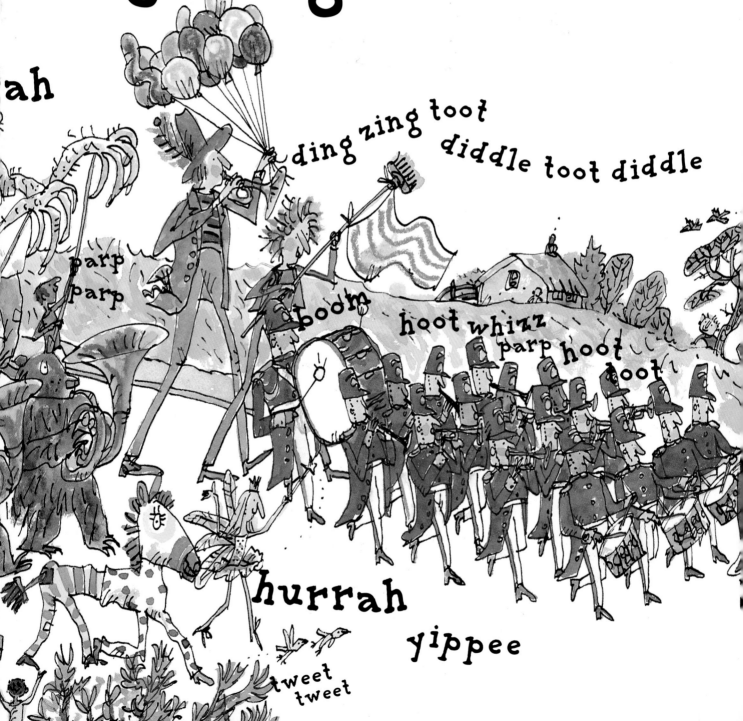